This is dedicated to Peggy, Jo, Smiley W and his family as without their inspiration this book would not have been written.
-Samantha Madison Langley

With Love From Smiley W. by Samantha Madison Langely Distributed by BookBaby 7905 N. Crescent Blvd.
Pennsauken, NJ 08110

Cover and Illustrations by Spectra T.

ISBN: 978-1-54397-447-8

Table of Contents

The Smiley W

Sometimes the heavens send us a gift. It can come in many different packages. This is the story of the coming of a little dog who has many challenges but is blessed with a pure heart—a heart with such a wonderful bright light that it touched all who knew him. This is the story of Smiley W, his family, and all who loved him.

Megan, sitting by the poolside with a restaurant on the other side of a door in the distance, held a little dachshund like a baby in her arms. He seemed to enjoy the attention. A breeze lightly came up, and he twisted as if following it. As the door to the restaurant opened, Smiley raised his head and looked directly at the lady passing through it.

"May I please see your little guy?" she asked. Megan sat amazed as Smiley reacted as if he not only saw her but heard her as well.

"He is absolutely adorable," the lady continued. "What is his name?" Megan looked stunned, which puzzled the lady, so she asked, "Is everything ok?"

Answering all three of the lady's queries at once, Megan replied,
"Yes, his name is Smiley, and you can definitely see him. Could you please do me a favor? Could you walk back to the door and then come back?"

"Sure." Now the lady was the one who looked puzzled, but she went ahead and did as requested.

Just as before, Smiley's head perked right up and he looked directly at the lady. Megan was again taken back and not sure what to make of it. She told the lady,

"I'm sorry for acting so strange, but Smiley is both deaf and blind. He is a very special little creature. He loves everybody and everything, but he lives in a bubble from sight and sound. The fact that he is reacting to your presence is astounding. I am not sure what to make of it."

"I'm Sharon from New York," replied the lady. "My husband is in town for a medical procedure. It is so beautiful here, but I just said to my husband that I miss hugging a pup! My Feona is at home, and I haven't left her for any amount of time in quite a while. We are leaving in three hours to fly home. I guess I'll always be addicted to dogs! Maybe that's why your dog senses me. Bill says that I must have been a dog in my past life!" She laughed as she recounted her husband's conclusion.

Megan explained that she had taken Smiley on vacation with her while she accompanied her partner on a work trip during which she was also going to look for new orchid venues.

"May I please take some pictures of you under the tree?" Sharon asked. "I would like to remember you and Smiley."

"Of course you can and would you do me a favor? Would you please hold Smiley? I would like to see his reaction to you. I'll take your picture with him."

By that time, Sharon's husband, David, was there was enjoying this little creature immensely. An amazing thing happened. When Sharon held Smiley, he looked right up into her eyes and nuzzled her. She had a far-off, very stunned look as tears started rolling down her cheeks as she felt a feeling that she couldn't describe. She held him and held him. She was speechless, but as she cooed to Smiley he continued to fixedly gaze into her eyes.

The Whitley Orchid Farm

It was 6:00 a.m., and the air smelled of the sweet smell of orchids, fresh green grass, and the morning dew on the plants. It was sunny and warm already.

"The flowers should be up by now and ready for their water. Terri is coming in this morning for her new job as my assistant, and I should be ready for orchid customers," Megan said to Chocolate Bunny and Honey Bunny, her two cocker spaniels who were obviously in dreamland. Sleepily, the two raised their heads.

"Are you two coming, or are you going to sleep all day? Breakfast is out in the green-house today!" Chocolate Bunny started shaking his head with his furry ears flopping.

"Not again," he groaned. "Can't we EVER sleep late?"

"Not if you want to eat and get cookies today," replied Megan as she could read his lazy groan.

Honey Bunny, who was totally into her beauty sleep, stretched her front legs and then the back ones and started to roll over and back to sleep. Chocolate was impatient and knew that

Megan would not wait forever for them to follow her.

"Honey, get up…. Liver and bacon cookies, remember? The customers always give us liver and bacon cookies at the flower house!"

Cookies, Honey Bunny thought sleepily. Cookies. Then finally she remembered the taste of liver and bacon…and became fully awake, exclaiming, "Yeah, cookies!"
With a burst of cookie thought energy, she sprang up, and the two dogs waddled out to the barn. Neither of their physiques seemed to have ever missed a meal.

Just inside the barn door was someone that absolutely loved the "Bunnies." They instantly knew that she was an easy touch and would be good for cookies all day.
"Oh, they're so beautiful!!" exclaimed Terry. "The dark brown and white is—?"

"Chocolate Bunny," Megan replied.

"And the one with the really pretty caramel color and white?"

"She is Honey Bunny" Megan responded. "Choco and Honey, come…. Meet Terri."
She really didn't have to call them, as the two were already on their way to the greenhouse aisle.

"Cookies, cookies, liver and bacon cookies!" the two dogs chanted.
After the official introduction that of course included petting and cooing and belly rubs, it was time to lie back down at the doorway.

Greenhouses are very special places. The dogs watched as Megan began showing Terri how to check and treat each flower. The houses were full of orchids. Orchids are an amazing plant and come in a rainbow of colors and shapes. Orchids are the flowers of kings and queens and, in Megan's case, of many wonderful friends that she had grown to know. The greenhouse was moist and the air was pure and warm. It smelled so good. There were potted plantings in rows and hanging from the ceilings. In the center were tables where Meg made magically beautiful arrangements to make people happy! This was a labor of love for Megan and she was the best to train Terri to watch over the greenhouse and even possibly do an arrangement or two. Everything from country to classical music played in the greenhouse while they worked, and they often sang along with the melodies.

After the greenhouse plants were taken care of, then the plants in the yard had to be watered before noon. To give both Bunnies their exercise, Megan called to them. With full bellies, however, both lazy pups lay in the aisle with the plants, neither wanting to move.

"Come on, you lazy pups. Up!" Choco got up with hesitation, but Honey said,

"Not me. The sun is too bright, and it bothers my eyes. There would be nothing as ugly as me with droopy eyes!"

Choco went over and insistently nudged her again and again:
"Get up! At least it is not raining and muddy and mucky! Then we would have to have a bath, and I hate baths. You are never happy—and totally a little priss." Honey glared at him.

"At least if it were raining, I would be able to get a bath and bathe in warm bubbles! I love playing with bath toys and being pampered. I love the blow-dryer and brushes and

Mom Meg cooing over me and saying that I am a real glamour-puss." Honey moseyed outside to help with the watering, but not very happily.

"Thank God, they finally went outside!" squeaked a little grey field mouse that considered himself the housemaid. He ran over to the dish to see if there were any morsels he should vacuum up. Finding a tiny piece of kibble that Honey had left under the rim of the dish, he seemed satisfied as he took the morsel up to his corner and made it go away.

"Those totally dumb pups don't even know I am here. Scruff runs this place. I climb high, run low, and will outrun them for sure." Scruff, as he named himself, took ownership of his surroundings.

The greenhouse was preparing to have an orchid show, and Honey and Chocolate weren't left out. Megan artfully made woven collars with baby's breath and orchids. Honey loved the attention of being a flower child.

"Don't I look pretty? So pretty? Well, what do you think? Huh, Huh?" She begged for an answer.
Choco glanced over at the prancing Honey and mumbled,

"Yeah, yeah. I hate these things. This is so embarrassing for a male like me. Flowers! Before you know it, I'll have bees around me! Yuck! This better get me lots of treats!"

The day went by, and before they knew it, the flowers were gone and things were back to normal. It was worth it, as they even received beef jerky as a thank you treat.

"Boy, was that good." Choco groaned with a solidly full stomach after downing a hefty serving of the jerky.

That night, Megan made dinner for all of them, and they lay on the floor in the living room, one on each side listening intently as she sang and wrote her music. This was the regimen they followed every night that the dogs so looked forward to because of the total attention that it garnered them. Their little family was perfect.

A New Addition

Terri came into work at the greenhouse one morning and mentioned that there was a dachshund named Tugs that really needed a home. He was scheduled to go to the shelter. So after the farm closed for business for the day. Maggie decided to go with Terri to see Tugs.

Coming to the "Overlook Dachshunds" sign, Megan was anxiously awaiting seeing the boy. The place was quite dirty and the man who had charge of Tugs was a grumpy person.

"If you want him, he's yours," he told them. "I have had enough. He bred my other dachshund, and now she is going to have an unwanted litter of pups. He is for immediate adoption."

Megan and Terri felt sorry for his dogs. Megan entered the back kennel, and Tugs sat in the corner. As the ladies watched him, he also was watching them.

"Oh great, I wonder what they want. They're watching me. I just know that this guy wants to be rid of me. I can feel it. Oh, boy. Oh BOY. I hope they're not the dog catchers! I don't like cages." Tugs muttered anxiously to himself.

Megan kneeled on the floor in front of him and just sat quietly. Tugs cocked his head from one side to another, trying to figure her out. Megan began to speak oh so softly to him.

"Hi, Baby Tugs. You are such a handsome man." She put out her hand with a cookie and just left it quietly by him. He was timid, but the cookie and the soft voice won him over. Soon he was sitting quietly by her side, and she was lightly petting him. After a while, he inched his way to her lap and laid his chin on her knee.

The man nodded in silent affirmation that Tugs was Megan's if she wanted him. He was just happy to see the dog go. The bond between Tugs and Megan had been formed, and Megan was to be his person. Most people do not know this truth, but a dog really does choose his person. When that happens, the bond cannot be broken, and the dog is forever loving and loyal to the person he has chosen. What Tugs did not know right then, however, is that there were other pups of the doggie family that he was about to meet and that he was going to have to learn to share.

When Tug got to his new home, he met Honey and Chocolate. He was much smaller than they were, and Choco in particular towered over him. The very large chocolate cocker made it known that he was the head of the dog kingdom at Beautiful Blooms.

Honey, on the other hand, met Tugs and thought he was sweet. "I don't know, Choco, but I think that he is adorable and even a little handsome!". Choco mumbled,

"He is not handsome. He looks like a hot dog on legs."

Tugs stayed to himself and the first day thought this might not be the best family he could have. He was not ready for these big, furry creatures, especially the dark brown one that growled at him. Feeling a little intimidated, Tugs slept on his new person's bed that night. He snuggled next to her on the pillow and dreamt of all the fun things that they would do together. Choco and Honey lay nose to nose at the foot of the bed together Choco was   displaced from his pillow by this new dog in the house.

"Handsome? Huh? You see where he is sleeping? Yuck! I hope he goes home soon." Honey didn't appear to hear him, as she was already stretched out asleep and breathing on his nose.

Megan knew that being the third one of anything was difficult, so she made Tugs her special baby. She hated to see him outside the Bunnies' clique. Sometimes when she was too busy to give him this extra special attention, his eyes looked so sad. Even though three dogs was already a lot, she was thinking of adding a fourth to the family. Would four dogs really be so bad? Even if she decided to go ahead and add a fourth one, she knew she might have to wait, because not only did she want another dachshund but she wanted to be sure to get a female.

Interestingly, Terri had an idea: "Overlook Dachshunds. He said that he had the female with the unwanted litter. Who knows? Maybe he will let her go."

Without hesitation, she and Megan made the call to the grumpy man who had given them Tugs, feeling that all the dogs would be better off adopted.

The grumpy old man, whose name was actually Chance Newson, answered in about one ring. "Hello…. Who is this?" they heard on the other end of the line.

"It's Megan and Terri. We adopted Tugs."

"NO, absolutely not, I am not taking him back. You can do what you want with—" Megan interrupted without taking a breath:

"No, NO, we do not want to give him back. We would like to see what you wish to do with the female that you mentioned with the unwanted litter. Has she delivered?"

"She didn't deliver yet," Chance answered. "The two are related, and she is also a disappointment. You can have her now for all I care."
This was unbelievable to Megan and Terri. Megan could have the dog now—but with puppies? It didn't take long for Megan to make her decision. She would go see the girl and find homes for the puppies after they were born.

Driving back to the kennel, they walked in to see Chance. "Come back here and you can see her," he beckoned to them.
Megan and Terri walked over to him and looked down at this poor little girl in the cage that was really much too small to give her the exercise that she needed. "She must be so crippled feeling in this small area with a delivery to come," Megan said.

"Yes, probably, she's due in about two weeks," Chance responded. "By the way, she is also deaf. One more strike against her. No one wants a deaf dog to breed, and I am not going to support a dog that does not produce. Besides that, she is not correct. Her color is wrong."

Most breeders will try to find a home for a misfit. Knowing that this person standing in front of her was obviously not the kind to spend his time to help any animal, Megan felt she was meant to be there and also glad that he was willing to give the dog to a good home.

The dog was so precious. She was mostly black with a white shawl around her neck and a beautiful tan nose. Megan had melted on sight. It only took a second before she came over and peeked at Megan through the mesh of the cage. Megan opened the door and picked her up and decided that she was going home now.

Chance stopped her at the door and started to say, "If you want the papers…"

"No, that won't be necessary," Megan interrupted, "as I do not want to breed her. She will be a family member. We have no use for papers at the farm. It is just not important to us."

"Well, if you want to buy the crate…"

"No, my dogs don't live in crates, but thank you." Megan and Terri left with the little girl, and Megan told her, "It doesn't matter what others think. I am going to cherish you." With that, Cherish became the new dog's name.

Cherish was a kind and lovely little dachshund with the biggest heart. Riding home, she lay on Megan's lap and cuddled against her waist, feeling the warmth of her new person. The bond had formed between the two, and now she would meet the rest of the family.

Upon arriving at the house, Megan brought Cherish into the kitchen. The cockers looked at her curiously. "Are you really one of us? You look so weird!" Choco couldn't help but ask.

Honey, being the diva, said, "Really!? But she seems to look like Tugs!" Cherish wondered what a Tugs was. "You look like you were caught in the ringer washing machine!" she added. "And you have no beautiful curls!"

Cherish felt saddened but stood and told them boldly, "I am going to someday have very special children that will all look like me, and they will be absolutely, positively amazing!"

The two Bunnies laughed and said, "We shall see."

Then Cherish found someone that looked like her. She crept slowly to the couch and sniffed and sniffed. Something smelled very familiar. In fact, she knew Tugs. Tugs raised his head with his eyes still half closed. He slowly sniffed back. He rolled off the couch and wandered around the room, following close behind Cherish. Now she had met the whole family.

Although Cherish was relieved to have found a familiar Tugs in her new home, she still felt outside the group until one day she found Scruff, the resident mouse, who had crept into Honey's dish. Cherish found that to be a real problem. "Get out of her food!" she cried.

With that, Cherish chased the mouse and dug and dug in the pots looking for him, scratching and pawing and knocking over piles of pots rolling in the aisle of the greenhouse

"Wait till Mom sees that!" Honey laughed to Choco. "She may be finding a new home sooner than she thinks!" Next came the pots with plants. In the meantime, Scruff was running down the backside of the glass wall and into the yard.

"Whew!" he exclaimed. He was not used to being chased by a dog. "I thought only cats chased people like me! That doesn't look like a cat! That doesn't look like me. It doesn't look like the Bunnies either."

Bunny walked slowly over, as she would never chase a mouse. That was a cat's job.

"Hey, why do you like to do that?" she asked Cherish.

Cherish answered proudly, "That is what we do. Dachshunds like us are hound types that flush out varmints—and rabbits and anything that burrows!"

"Well, then, I guess you will be of use here after all.," Honey replied.

Suddenly Cherish had found her place in the family. She could do something that the cockers could not. She and Honey became friends, as Honey knew the value of having her food saved! And Scruff knew that either he had to make Cherish his friend or he might be in big trouble. He might even end up very hungry or possibly even her dinner!

The greenhouse looked like a hurricane hit the aisle, and pots were all over. Terri came into the greenhouse and looked at the mess. Shaking her head, she looked from dog to dog and asked,

"Who did this?"

This time, the dogs hung together, as they had found a mutual interest. All four looked and twisted their heads in wonder and gazed at her with total innocence. Unfortunately for them, it was easy to tell the one who had done the bad deed! She was covered with the potting soil and still had a pot on her head!

In the meantime, Megan came in and could not help but laugh along with Terri when

"Huddle...we're in trouble now!"

they saw Cherish pawing at her head to remove the plastic pot. The dachshunds would be a handful, Megan realized, but she knew that they would be worth it.

The cockers and dachshunds stayed in their own groups, and Tugs became the little boy that was totally spoiled by the ladies. Megan engaged all of them in play later in the afternoon. She threw the ball for them to go chase it down, and the dogs seemed to love it! She laughed and laughed as the little hot dogs ran as fast as their little legs could move and the cockers ran past them with no effort. Soon the difference in ages began to show, though, and Honey and Choco lay down to rest. Tugs and Cherish joyfully continued to chase the ball. Scruff sat on greenhouse trim, watching them.

"Oh, why did she get another dog? I will never be able to steal the food from those hot dogs! What's a mouse to do?" he moaned to himself. Tugs and Cherish were just too happy with their person's attention to worry about chasing Scruff now.

After their long romp, Cherish was even feeling tired. She could not get comfortable.. Meg thought it was from all of the trouble she had been in during the day. Her belly was huge, and she looked so uncomfortable. From the day Cherish appeared, Tugs claimed her as his and became the head of his small dog family. Tugs was about three years old and thought that he would like being a dad. He did not enjoy the role of fatherhood. Cherish, for her part, was the perfect momma. She proudly showed the new puppies to anyone who would look. Megan was amazed at these tiny little creatures that were no bigger than small mice. There was one puppy that stood out from the crowd. He was a whitish spotted puppy with absolutely the biggest ears! As the weeks passed, he became full of personality. Honey said,

"Boy, they are strange. Are they really dogs like us? They look like Scruff."

Scruff was a very curious mouse. "What do you mean they look like me?" he wondered. Scruff stayed outside the house door as long as it was warm. On the cold nights, the dogs would see him creeping over the counters and bark to alarm the little thief, but Scruff was so fast that he had never been caught by them.

Meg would laugh at the dogs, "He is just too fast for you!" Scruff could not help but try to see these little creatures that the Bunnies claimed resembled him.

Choco said, "Yeah, they are strange alright....Look at that white one with black spots and the one that is colored like you but has no hair! And that one with the ears, he really is a misfit!"

The little dog with the big ears was not upset by the statement. He would wake up with the biggest smile on his face, always screaming to the group, "I am here and I love my life!" and the smiles were contagious. Megan was drawn to this little white spotted pup with the crazy big ears even though he also had just one good eye.

Cherish loved all her babies but knew that they all had health problems. Moms just sense these things. Dogs are forgiving, though, and make the best of life as it is. This was the case with these babies, and thank God they were born to a very special home. It was the home of Megan Whitley and her Orchid Farm. Meg also had a sense that there were health and physical shortcomings.

Ten weeks into their life, she visited the veterinarian. Upon completing the examination of all these puppies, the veterinarian came in with a sad look on his face and told Megan,

"Aren't they beautiful, Tugs?!"

"I believe that it would be in the best interest of these puppies to end their lives. Two of them are deaf, one is blind in one eye and deaf, one has a heart problem, and one has a lung problem. All of these things will surely be a problem for both them and you."

Megan, while very sad, knew her decision. "How long do you feel these puppies will live? Is this a matter of handicaps or life?"

The veterinarian spoke in the kindest voice, "It will be hard to tell. The handicaps give them a harder life, and it is much easier for them to become injured it they are blind. Not being able to hear can make them not know of things that can hurt them. The heart is an unknown issue. A heart can beat for years or just stop."

Megan listened and left the veterinarian's office having decided that she would ponder this. The puppies started to grow and they were happy as they were. When you are blind from birth, it is a normal state of affairs to you. Being blind in only one eye should be workable. When you are deaf, the world can have a wonderful peacefulness. All of these shortcomings can be overcome. In any case, the puppies came to communicate between themselves with Momma Cherish, Pop Tugs, and the Bunnies all not caring that they were different. Megan knew the differences and hesitated to name them, as time would only tell their future. One thing was certain: She was not going to end their lives due to their handicaps. She took it upon herself to continually hold the long-eared pup. There was just something about him. It was absolutely hysterical to watch him, as his ears were so long that he would sometimes trip over them. The others would all laugh. She picked him up, and he still had the most incredible smile on this face that never left. With his one good eye gazing directly at Megan, she suddenly knew his name.

"You are Smiley…. You are Smiley W for Smiley Wonderful," she told him. This sweet dog, with a personality bigger than life reached up to her and licked her face. Now the Smiley dog had his name.

Momma Cherish took it upon herself to tend the group, and it was amazing how the puppies with blindness, deafness, and other ills settled into the house like a normal family. Other than in the case of Smiley, Megan had not named the puppies yet. She realized that it was time, but the names came slowly, as she wanted to name the puppies for their real personalities. For example, the little girl puppy was a prissy little thing with an air about her that was very regal. She was like a little princess, and her markings were very classy.

Megan said, She is actually cocoa- and white-colored and looks like a designer's creation. After smelling the Chanel #5 that the little one had spilled over the floor, it was a given. She would be named Coco Chanel. Smiley introduced her to the pack: "Oh, wow, she stinks!" He was determined to make everyone laugh.

He added, "Come on guys, let's play. It's a beautiful day." You could watch him speak to the others with his contagious smile that made you smile the minute you saw him. Choco looked at him, wondering,

"Why are you always smiling? Are you a dummy? You can't even hear me, so why do I bother speaking to you?"

Smiley's smile widened, and all his senses told him that Choco was trying to get his attention. Loudly, he barked and yipped and wagged his tail, and the long ears flapped in the breeze. Megan looked at them curiously, knowing that they were communicating somehow. Grey Boy was a handsome pup and bigger than Smiley. He had the most beautiful blue-grey

"Now it's perfect. I'm here!"

coat with a white chest. He even had normal ears. The trouble with Grey Boy was his heart. It had a murmur. The little Smiley boy, who could see with his one good eye, thought how handsome his brothers were. One day he wandered through the house with his siblings and caught a look of this very funny thing that was looking back at him. He barked and barked. He looked to the left and saw Oreo and then saw Honey Bunny on the other side.

"Oh my gosh, that is me!" he exclaimed. He then really knew the size of his ears. He soon became closest to his black and white brother whom Megan had named Oreo, after the cookie. One day a neighbor was visiting and was spending time with the largest of the puppies. He was a real handful and adored Megan, but he was also a real challenge. He was bold and loud and demanding. The visiting customers laughed at him constantly. He would not be ignored and used every opportunity to get attention. He would bark, but at a different tone than his sister and brothers. He used that bark to demand attention.
The neighbor looked at his stance and markings and said,

"He sounds like he's mooing!" She laughed and that was it. He was now MooMoo. Smiley seemed to love that name, as he reacted by jumping on him, yipping and trying to see what the "mooing" was about.

The kids played and played. They were the entertainment committee and could make a person laugh on the darkest day. Megan found herself lost in time watching these very special, challenged pups interacting. Months passed, and the farm was in full bloom with a large variety of flowers. Of course, there was now daily entertainment from Smiley and the rest of the gang, which made people laugh and come back if only just to see the dogs. The little bit of work they caused Megan from their mischief was well worth the fun they created during the day. Smiley, for example, used his super-sized ears to make the children notice him

No one ever left the farm without a smile on his or her face. The Bunnies still sat like statues at the entrance to the greenhouse, as the welcoming committee.

Tugs saw the "Bunnies" as a strange breed. "Look at all those waves and curls. Spots that don't match. I find hair bunnies all over the house! Hey, hair bunnies! I bet that's why they named them Bunnies! Ha ha ha!" he chuckled. "What do you think, Cherish?"

"Yes, they may be different, but we're all different. Who's to say what's right? We are all family. There are no bullies in this house, and no one judges each other, and we all know our place."

Tugs eventually became a problem with his boys. He would growl out loud, "Just go to a corner and stay there," as he pushed and nipped at the puppies until they conformed. At first it seemed like he was training them, and then there was doubt on Megan's part as to whether this was normal. He seemed to be growling much too much. After the group got chastised by their dad, very slowly, the cute little puppy with the big ears and wide grin came over and lay down at Megan's feet. He looked up at her and barked loudly.

"And what would you like?" she asked him. Although he could not hear her, he responded with a yip and a wagging tail and one little front paw very gently placed on her shin. It was impossible not to pick him up. She looked at him as he curled up, burying his face in her neck. He immediately gave a little sigh as he went to sleep with dreams of running through the fields with his Momma Cherish, Momma Meggi, and, of course, Oreo. Megan realized that she had been blessed with these wonderful dogs that wanted only to make her happy. They loved her—and loved her and loved her. She lay on the couch with the puppy at her neck and woke up a few hours later, as she felt him move softly. Opening her eyes, she saw that he was staring directly into her eyes with the sweetest look and that wonderful smiley face. "You definitely are Smiley. And you couldn't be more wonderful." she told him.

And Smiley he was. Wonderful he would always be. Smiley always devoted his time to Megan, and every other living creature that he could feel wanted his attention. He was so many things. He was the little devil. He was the little angel with ears for wings! He was the clown. He would run through the greenhouse and carry whatever orchid he could reach that day. Some days they were orange, and some days they were white with beautiful purple centers—and he loved the birds of paradise. The bright colors looked like a flag as he ran through the greenhouse trying to draw attention. He would come down the aisle covered with potting soil, shaking his ears and watching as the soil floated through the air. He was a carefree little hotdog, and sometimes he made his way into the flower arrangements just to peek through at the customer as if to say, "Now this arrangement is really perfect! I'm in the middle of it!"

He rapidly became the puppy that everyone was drawn to. Those big ears made him irresistible to the customers. The farm should have been named Smiley Orchids, as he virtually became the face of the farm. Scruff looked curiously at him and said, "What exactly are those ears?" They became Smiley's trademark.

Tugs grew angrier by the day. This was HIS family and HIS friends and HIS greenhouse. "The patio, the house and the flowers…. They are mine and Cherish's. Why did she have to have these kids?" he muttered to himself. Of course, the Bunnies would also be here, and he could not challenge them. But he knew that Oreo and Smiley were just getting too much attention. Tugs barked and growled and threatened the boys: "These are my people, my girls.

Stay away!"

Oreo knew to stay away, as he could hear the growls and sense Tugs's anger. Sometimes Tugs would nip at his neck or shoulder as a reminder. Smiley, however, was still getting just too much attention and this drove Tugs crazy. He did not know how he could have had such an annoying son. The ears that he always made fun of became Smiley's most adorable point. One day Tugs pushed Smiley, and he did not move. Tugs jumped on Smiley, attacking him, and the next thing anyone knew, Smiley was at the veterinary hospital. The vet checked several bites Smiley had received, but he was most worried about Smiley's one eye. The next morning when Smiley awoke, he whined because the side of his face was burning. He asked the others, "Why is it so dark here today? I can't see you guys!"

Coco Chanel said warily, "Smiley, go back to sleep. The sun is out, and it is a beautiful day!"

Smiley repeated, now in a panicked whine. "Chanel, this is for real. I don't know what is wrong with me. It's still dark in here! Help!" as he tripped clumsily into the corner table. Smiley W was now totally blind. Megan was devastated and knew that something had to be done with Tugs. From that day, Smiley was her chosen baby, as she became his eyes.

The smile, however, was still on Smiley's face. "It's okay, Momma. God gave me time to see you all and know how beautiful the farm is. I can remember now. You are the most beautiful mom. I love my Meggi's smile and how her eyes glisten when she looks at me. I remember Terri and Meggie dancing strangely through the greenhouse to little vibrations that tickled my butt. That's what MooMoo calls music! Coco is the beauty puss, and Honey, well, she has the most beautiful curls on caramel fur! And I know about caramels, as I stole some out of the candy jar! I can still see MooMoo, my Oreo, and the handsome Grey Boy. I can feel the warmth of the sun. I remember what it is —and the flowers and even Scruff. I still am here, and I can picture you all. It's all good."

"Meggi," as Smiley called her, could feel his words as she felt the tears coming down her face. It was strange how Smiley could make you hear him and know how he felt. Smiley knew how you felt, too. People realized that Smiley was a very special angel. From that time on, Choco Bunny and Honey Bunny made it their purpose to discipline Tugs whenever he went near the boys. This bully now felt what it was like to be bullied. Tugs would turn, and Choco would turn faster. One day in the greenhouse, Tugs decided to turn and nip at Choco, which was a BIG mistake. HUGE! Tugs ended up with a patch of Choco's long fur in his mouth that he then breathed in and felt what it was like to choke and choke. Choco turned around and grabbed him firmly and dragged him the length of the greenhouse. Terri was amazed at the fact that Choco actually never hurt him. He just put him in line. Something had to change this; the customers could not see these dogs squabbling.

One day, Tugs finally found a customer who adored him, a girl who especially came to see him, and he seemed to love her. He had found a one-pup person, and now he could have all the attention he
wanted. Megan hated to lose him, but the bond between Tugs and the girl was unmistakable. So Megan gave a party on the patio for everyone at the farm, including the girl, giving the dogs time to both meet Tugs's new master and play. After that, Tugs enjoyed play dates with the dogs whenever the girl came to buy orchids at the farm or just to visit.

The flowers flourished. The farm's business grew, and there were lots of customers with children to play with the pups. They ran around the outside yard and looked forward to coming. It became a weekly outing. The Whitley Orchid farm was the place to be! The days were filled with fun and treats, and Cherish had a natural way of babysitting all the children. The dogs had their everyday routine, which dogs love, and everyone settled into his life. The Bunnies were also happy dogs. Dreamland was fun now, too, as all seven dogs would lie in a pile next to their person. At the Orchid farm, the life of a dog was good. It had not taken long until the seven of them played as before Smiley's accident and the house became the Animal Kingdom.

The customers loved all the pups, and Smiley still seemed to be constantly in mischief and always the center of attention. He made everyone laugh as he came running down the aisle with a pile of pots or tried to jump on the table like the bunnies and ended up falling in the compost bag while Megan was busy doing the arrangements. Many times he would forget his route and run into something with a thump. Megan would always cringe when this happened, wondering if he was hurt, but he took everything in stride. He was a clown. Megan realized that because Smiley was deaf and blind, he had developed an uncanny sense of knowing when people or other living things were hurting. He seemed to gravitate toward those people who seemed sad, and he never ceased to make them smile. Everyone settled in to their routines, including the cockers, who would sit and have their morning nap in the greenhouse. The dachshunds now had outside watering detail after breakfast. Honey Bunny said sleepily on a warm Saturday morning, "Well, Choco, we've come a long way. We can relax now. Finally, we will be treated like royalty."

"Honey, where have you been?" Choco responded. "You've always been treated like royalty!"

The pups loved their lives, and Megan made sure that they were spoiled. The orchids were in bloom, and the business was steady. It boomed on special occasions when loved ones wanted to remember each other. Valentine's Day was for lovers and close friends. Mother's Day was to let your mom know how much you loved and appreciated her. Everyone should show their caring and appreciation. The dogs showed it, too! They took a number of the potted plants, playing with them as they went, and left them in a pile for Meg and Terri. Unfortunately, Megan found them by tripping over the pile and ended up flat on the floor in the greenhouse.

"Oh my gosh! I think we are in BIG trouble now! All we wanted to do was bring her presents!" the dogs said to each other, and they all immediately ended up on top of Megan, giving her the biggest sloppy wet wash she could imagine. They snuggled and snuggled to let her know that they were sorry and to make their person feel better. She looked at the pile, no longer perfectly stacked, and then at them and sensed what they were doing, as dogs bring presents to their owners for praise. She could not help but laugh and hug them all.

"This is what having a family really is, isn't it, you crazy little pups!"

And there was always music playing at the farm, especially on the holidays. Meg and Terry would bop around to the music, and the dogs just had to join them. The group put on their own show, just for themselves.

Martha

One day Meg's mom, Martha, came to visit. Martha loved animals and while her love of the Bunnies had always been a constant, she was instantly enamored with the little dachshunds that were new to the pack. Megan loved to watch her with the pups. Cherish, in particular, seemed to take possession of Martha, as she curled up and lay quietly at Martha's side. It was great for Megan to have help with the evening dinners and company to spend the nights with. Martha loved sitting in the yard breathing in the fragrance of the flowers. The light would shine through her silver hair neatly pinned in a bun, and she would sit in a rocking chair reading the latest novel on the best seller list. The gardens were lush with so many different plants and flowers. Megan would set up a table near the patio and bring the flowers for the arrangements for her mom to help set things up. Terri had learned to take care of the orchids, and now she began trying to make the arrangements and do the deliveries. Each pot surrounding the patio looked as it is was part of a picture book. They were carefully and artfully placed not only to serve as eye candy but also to provide calming, sweet fragrances for the nose.

Cherish spent more and more time with Martha, and Honey Bunny also started hanging at her feet. Megan noticed this and thought it was a little strange, but she wrote it off to the fact that her mom was the one able to give them the most attention. She also wondered how often

"Grandma, we love you!"

her mom was feeding them treats. Smiley also became very attached to Martha and could often be found lying quietly on her lap, asleep for hours.

Martha, still full of fun, was aging, and it takes a canine to really understand this and the ills that a person feels. A person's pup will understand and comfort them much before any human can realize that there's even a problem. It took the pups to bring something to light about Martha that Martha hadn't even known.

One day after breakfast, they all went out on the terrace to lounge in the sun. Suddenly the loud noise of the fire alarm was going off! The dogs ran in circles, barking madly and generally carrying on. Megan and Terri heard the alarm from where they were in the greenhouse, and by the time they got to the kitchen door, the smoke was billowing through the windows. The fire had started in a pan with a rag on the stove that Martha had forgotten was there. She was beyond upset and shaking and apologizing to Megan as she cried.

This was a turning point in Martha's health. Days went by when she would forget Meg's name. What day it was. Where she left her glasses. The way to go outside. Whether she had breakfast or not. Megan was devastated to see her mom in this condition. It hurt her terribly when her mom did not remember her name. Although she already knew what the diagnosis would be, she took her mom to the doctor all the while praying there was something minor going on instead of the diagnosis she dreaded hearing. The doctor, after running many tests, came into the examination room and uttered the diagnosis that Megan had been dreading:

"Your mom has ALZHEIMERS." Actually hearing the diagnosis was like hitting a brick wall, because Alzheimer's disease is known as the "forgetting disease" and is incurable. Megan took her mom back to the farm, knowing that her mom would never go back to her own home again.

She spoke to Martha while making dinner that night:

"Mom, I really can use you help here. If you were to leave, all of the children would miss your company, and I would have no one to play my guitar for in the evening. Also, I desperately need your help babysitting the little Smiley man." she added. Her mom, always trying to help her daughter, did not hesitate to offer to stay and help.

Later that evening, Smiley, Cherish, Choco, and Honey all lay beside Martha. Coco, MooMoo, and Grey Boy lay by Meg nearest the food dish. Megan realized that her beloved pups had known there was a problem even before she did. Looking back at the past few weeks, she realized they had been particularly affectionate with her mom and had stayed right by her side. This being a long-term illness for her mom, Megan came to depend upon Terri to cover the business and spent most of her time beside her mom. She wanted to spend every waking minute with her, knowing that someday her mom might not remember her.

As time went on, she became a coach and a caregiver for Martha. The dogs would lie right beside them. When the days were bleak and sometimes tears fell, they would come over and give lots of kisses to wash the tears away. Martha always giggled whenever Smiley became intent on licking her entire face, and she never forgot his name.

"Smiley W, am I that dirty?" she'd ask, and Smiley seemed to respond to her. Every once in a while, Smiley and the gang would do something outrageous to make them laugh.

Martha still enjoyed the flowers and the gardens and found a true bond with the tiny things that made her happy. She retreated to a time in her life when she was young and things were wonderful. One of the only good things about the forgetting disease is that you sometimes go to a time or a dream that makes you very happy. Once in a while, Meg would come in and find her mom in her own world. She would greet Meg as though she were a teenage friend and dance around the house singing merrily and even get into the makeup. She would be at the Chez' Noire, and she was Ginger Rogers and she was dancing with Fred Astaire. Or was she J. Lo and dancing with Simon Cowell? Whomever it was, she was humming and radiant. For Meg, that was bittersweet, as her mom was enjoying a time that she must have dreamed of years ago. In those moments, Martha was happy. Megan never lost hope of a time when there would be a cure for the forgetting disease.

For three years, Martha lived amidst those who loved her the most. In spite of her forgetfulness, she found joy in the faces of Smiley and Cherish and Choco and Honey. She laughed when they wagged their tails so hard that they knocked something off the little table by her wheelchair. The farm was still in bloom, but the cost of Megan's care for mom and time spent away from the business started to show. The buildings were showing wear, and as much as Megan trained Terri, it took a special talent to make the magical arrangements that Megan was known for producing. The love that had previously gone into planting was just not there, because all of Megan's love went to her mom now. The concerns regarding bills and business were trival and not of importance to her.

The days and months passed. Bills piled up and were left unopened—except by Moo-Moo, who usually found them as great playtime pieces. One day MooMoo and Cherish decided to make their people smile. The house looked like it had snowed whenever a stack of bills fell, and this was fun! Scruff made his way into the house, as he was lonely outside. That was the beginning of the game. As Scruff jumped from counter to counter, the hot dogs

would try to reach him.

"Cherish, get the Scruff!" Honey would bark. "Come on, MooMoo, you want to help?"

This motivated Cherish to find the way to rid the house of this rodent forever! The counters were just too high until…. Cherish and MooMoo found a bench that led to the chairs and jumped to the counter. Scruff ran behind the jugs full of flour and sugar, and they followed. Their instincts took hold as they rooted through everything on the counter, but the dachshunds were just too fat to run behind the cannisters. The flour covered both dogs' faces and went all over the floor. Worse, Honey Bunny, much older and more sedate, scolded them as the flour and sugar landed on her, That furry coat sure did look funny full of flour!

"You are such bad dogs," she scolded them. "You rotten little hot dogs! How am I going to clean myself? I will not be blamed for your bad behavior!"

Then MooMoo and Cherish stopped and looked at each other, amazed "Wow, we all match now!" they exclaimed to each other. "We are all white dogs!"

Choco then ran past Honey with an envelope in his mouth, totally disregarding what she had to say. "Come and get it!" he told her. When she responded with disdain, he added, "Boy, no one wants to play these days. Lighten up, Honey Bunny…. You really look beautiful as a white dog!"

One day when Megan awoke, her mom did not want to get up. Martha did not want to eat. Smiley W stayed glued to her side for the day and then into the next. A fear of the future was evident with the family, and every noise echoed through them in fear that they would soon have to live without Grandma. She was getting older and her forgetful disease had taken its toll on her. She was tired. She was so proud of Megan. She knew that no matter what life would bring, her daughter had the means and the character to choose her priorities wisely. She had watched Megan tend to the flowers and grow into the most talented person she had ever known. She had never believed that she would have a daughter that could compose such beautiful music, write poetry only to dream of, and grow such beautiful flowers—and more than that, have a heart so big to take in this wonderful family that needed her.

Martha was tired and felt that she no longer had to fear for her daughter. She knew that she had done a good job in raising her daughter into a caring, lovable, very sensitive person. Knowing all of this, peaceful and content, Martha passed quietly over the bridge to heaven, awaiting the family that would someday join her.

Times...They Are A-Changin

The day came when Megan feared that she was going to lose her home and the farm she had worked so long for. The house that she had spent so many nights in, with all her memories of Martha and the dogs. The flowers and all the plants that she had lovingly planted and cared for all those years. Her business. They would come and liquidate her beloved orchids that she had given so much of herself to tending. Terri had to leave, as there was very little business anymore and thus no way to pay her any longer. But while Terri left the orchid farm and moved on, Megan could not. She looked around the house and the gardens that were so in need of work. Although the farm had lost its luster during the hard times, Megan had all those memories that she couldn't leave. She was drained now, and she seemed to know only how to cry. All she could realize was the great loss. The children lay by her side in the bed, giving endless comfort and licking the tears as they rolled down her cheeks. She knew that she had an incredible family left that would love her and that they would stay for their entire lives with her. Would that be enough? It would have to be.

As Megan sat in the house, she prayed for an answer:

What do I do?

She had belongings ready to pack in the van and her seven dogs. She had very little money left and soon might have no home. She prayed and prayed.

Change is inevitable, you must change with it

is the answer that she received in her heart and acknowledged. Afraid, but hoping that God would show her the way, Megan tried to pull it together and realized that she should be more like her beloved pups. Challenged since birth, they nevertheless thrived through their challenges.

With their example as her model, Megan decided to go non-stop and give her all to her four-legged family and her work. The things that her mother had told her she began to live by: "Work is not work if you are doing what you love. Never cease to express yourself. You are a very talented lady with much to give the world. God gave you these children, and they will be your salvation no matter what else happens in your life."

Megan remembered these truisms every time she doubted the future. She thanked God for having had a mother like Martha and for giving her the family of loving little creatures that colored her life during this period. Martha's voice continued to echo in her mind with yet more wisdom for her:

"Megan, keep going. You are not alone. We'll always be here with you. Remember, you just have to believe."

The tears filled Megan's eyes as she realized that this was one of the last things her mom had said to her in minutes of lucidity before she died. Although she had heard this and always believed her mom, Megan was still afraid of the future now, knowing what it was like to feel a big hole in your heart and wonder if it would ever heal. Upon praying one night, she heard a voice say,

"Time will fill the hole with the warmth and memories of when you were together. Now you have your pups. I put on them on earth to love you and keep you strong."

The days were long now, and Meg was sad. Through all of her sadness, though, her four-legged children never missed a chance to sit around her, cradling her with their warm little bodies.

With all her push to get back to normal, while the business was growing, her family was shrinking. Poor little Grey Boy's heart stopped in his sleep. He went peacefully, and all his family was near to say goodbye.

"My brother was the most beautiful boy I ever saw," proclaimed Smiley. Though the farm's occupants filled with tears, they all knew that they would see him again. Dogs have that sense.

The orchid farm grew bigger and better, and the talent that Megan had was being realized by the neighboring communities. She took part in and exhibited her work at many of the prestigious orchid shows. She loved her poetry and played the guitar for the dogs at night. Even Smiley, who was now deaf and blind, seemed to sense the serenity of the music. Megan never knew whether it was a special sense that he had or that he related to the vibration of the music. It really didn't matter. He was happy, and his smile showed it.

As for MooMoo and Cocoa Channel, they were always challenging each other and full of mischief, but they calmed as they became older. The Bunnies were aging rapidly and became feeble, but they were still as young as ever to Smiley. He remembered them as they were when he could see. He would curl up next to them during the day, whether it be in the greenhouse or under a shade tree, and he would make it a point to introduce the Bunnies to children in his own way:

"These are my Bunnies. Aren't they beautiful? This is my Auntie Honey and Uncle Choco!! They are just like us, only bigger!"

Pictures of the group hung in the orchid showroom of the farm. Over the next year, both Bunnies would say goodbye to their family, and the loss would be immeasurable. Within months of each other, they passed and went up to be with Grey Boy. Smiley took the passing of the Bunnies harder than anyone. They had been closest to him, and he had loved lying on their long, wavy fur that was like a pillow to him. He missed the many times that Honey would lie next to him and decide to give him a bath with her tongue, being sure not to miss a bit of his face. The Bunnies, sensing that Smiley had gone totally blind, had become his eyes, and Honey Bunny had been the first one to protect him. Honey many times would tell Smiley in her own way,

"Little man, you won't ever get rid of me. I'll always be with you. You wait and see." They watched out for him. They would always seem to be in front of him at the steps, for example. Now Smiley was on his own.

Time had passed and, once puppies, they were nine years old now and preferred being couch potatoes, but Oreo and Smiley regained the bond that they first had as puppies in the litter. Smiley remembered Oreo as a puppy with the bold black and white markings. Smiley would watch Oreo intently as he rolled and grabbed his own ears and tried to pull on them.

"What are you doing? Is there something bothering you?" Smiley asked him one day.

"Yes, you fool, I want to have ears like yours!" Oreo told him. "If I pull on them enough, they may stretch and be long like yours!" Smiley remembered the biggest smile that he had ever felt that day. Oreo loved his ears! Imagine that!

Megan could not get over her many losses in the past couple of years. She began to realize that life was short. Some nights just before she fell asleep, she looked up to the sky, asking, "Mom, I want to believe. Are you still here for us?"

An answer always came back—"All you have to do is believe, Megan"—as her eyes began to close from a long day at work.

A New Dawn

One day, a beautiful lady came into the greenhouse to look for an arrangement. She had short hair and pretty brown eyes, and, most importantly, she absolutely adored the little hot dogs. Cocoa Chanel immediately climbed on her. The lady had apparently just come from work and was not really dressed for sitting on the ground, but when Megan came into the showroom, she found her sitting on the dirt, with the hot dogs all circling her. They were all vying for her attention. This was unusual for the pups, as customers had become the norm for them, and they usually were laid-back in their presence now. Megan felt very comfortable telling the lady each one's name. Then she said to the lady, "Now they would like to know your name."

"My name is Samantha, and you can call me Sam," said the lady.

"I am Megan Whitley, and you can call me Meg," Meg smiled in return.

It turned out that Sam had heard of the orchid lady and her talents. "So you really are the Megan Whitley that people call the 'orchid lady'?" she asked.

Megan then lit up when Sam couldn't help but tell her how well known her arrangements had become. "I wanted to stop by, as I have to go to a dinner party this evening and would like to bring something other than the typical wine," she told Megan.

Megan couldn't wait to show her all of the different arrangement options and took the time to give Sam a tour of the farm. Sam was clearly in love with the flowers and the dogs and even the property. She happily chose one of the arrangements Megan had shown her when they finished the tour. Megan wrapped up her choice, and, before leaving, Sam had to hold each of the hot dogs. "Someday, I will bring My Beau with me to meet your pups if it is ok with you," she told Megan.

Megan brightened, and so did Smiley. It was as if he knew. "Sure, anytime at all," Megan replied. After this initial meeting and introduction, Sam and her Beau—whom she brought with her the next time she visited the farm—spent much time at the farm, and The Beau fit in perfectly with the kids. Samantha loved the serenity of farming the orchids, the soothing sweet smells in the greenhouse, and the art of making the arrangements. She actually loved to be digging around in the potting soil!

"Being dirty feels good!" she laughed.

Soon Sam moved in with Megan and the pups, and they all became inseparable. Finally Megan had a person back in her life to share the joys and misfortunes that always come with living. She thanked God, as everything was complete again. Smiley was still the center of attention, and he was an extraordinary being. Almost everywhere they went, Smiley W. came with them. Wherever he was, and whoever he saw, he made an impact on people's lives. Smiley had a way of radiating joy to those who needed it. It became clear that Smiley W WAS special and this challenged little being was definitely God's little ambassador. There were so many times that he affected people, but Sam and Megan kept remembering the time when Smiley met Sharon from New York. They were convinced that Smiley could feel the need that someone had and react to it. Such a strong bond had formed between them and Sharon, but particularly with Smiley, in just 20 minutes. It was incredible. Many times after Megan and Sam's ensuing daily call with Sharon, they would ask the pup,

"Smiley, what did you sense? Did you like Sharon? Can you really see and hear? This has never happened before. We wish we knew what you were thinking and what kind of sense this is that you have at times."

It took some time, but the magic of that meeting with Sharon stayed with Megan. "Sam and I have been baffled by that morning, as he really did react to you and we believe that he saw you," Megan told Sharon on one of their daily calls.

The memory also mystified Sharon, who replied, "I have always believed it was more than that. Smiley had felt me and knew that I truly needed to hold him at that time. It was the first time I had been away from home since a vacation nine months before. I really have been against leaving my Feona, my older therapy dog. She has given so many people so much and has a wonderful spirit. Though it has been over nine months since the loss of her boy and our baby boy, Winston, she has had no closure and wanders the house looking for him. Animals experience loss much like we do and it may even be more intense for them. She is dependent upon us now and has separation anxiety. We had to come out to California for David's treatment. Although it was clear across the continent, it was the only center where we could get the stem cells he needed. That morning after the treatment, we were so relieved that it was over, but all the loss and fears just rushed in. As I sat in the restaurant, I was just aching inside. I thought of Feona being at home and needing us. I remembered my boy, the day I left, not knowing that those were the last sloppy kisses I would ever get from him. It was overwhelming. I knew when Smiley happened to be there at just that moment that he was a gift from God. I guess you can call him divine intervention. I will never be able to explain it, but Smiley is a very special being. I have never had the feeling rush over me that happened when Smiley was put in my arms. I never could understand the word "Joy," but if there is such a feeling, then I believe that is what I felt at the moment I held Smiley W. I believe that God put him on this earth for a very special purpose, and I am so blessed to have been able to hold him. I don't know if I will ever forget that feeling, it was a close as I have ever felt to a spirit. I wish that I could hold him every day and feel that magical feeling!"

After this heartfelt testimony from Sharon, the feeling that Megan always had about Smiley W was confirmed. Sharon became like an auntie to the family and called every day to see how they all were doing and to send hugs to the beautiful dog that she called her special angel.

Sam and Megan loved the beach, so many nights they would pack dinner and take the dogs to the ocean. Cherish loved it. MooMoo rolled in the sand. Coco Chanel hung out with Beau and did not like the feeling of wet fur. Smiley stayed close to Megan's heels and walked in her footsteps with ultimate trust. Life was good.

Before they knew it, time flew by. The kids were 10 years old, and The Beau was going to be 14. She was a very pretty little long-haired dog that actually was dwarfed by the hot dogs. She probably weighed 10 pounds, whereas MooMoo weighed over 40. She was definitely a priss and much like Coco in disposition. Their dispositions resembled cats, as The Beau pointed out:

"We are not put on this earth to pamper humans. If they want to pay attention to us, then they can come to us. We are delicate, lady-like dogs. This jumping and drooling and begging is beneath us, right Chanel?". This little BeauBeau had it all together. Coco just nodded in total agreement.

Smiley and Cherish both were showing signs of lameness. The little hot dogs are prone to spinal problems due to the length of the back torso that is unsupported. Cherish limped around. "I feel like a totally old lady now," she moaned. "Gee, my back hurts."

"Maybe it's because you are so overweight that the stress on the backbone is making you sway back!" commented an unsympathetic MooMoo.

"Look who is talking!" Cherish snapped back at MooMoo, who was definitely pudgy all over.
Smiley was gimpy, but he never seemed to complain. Megan and Sam treasured every minute with the kids, because they knew they would age fast. It was unimaginable to think of life without the hot dogs and Beau.

One evening Smiley begged to get on the bed, which usually was not allowed unless the humans were in the bed to cradle him. Once he was up on the bed this time, he immediately mis-stepped and fell blindly to the floor, where he lay whimpering and crying. The crying continued, and it pierced all of them. Smiley had never cried before, even during the problems with Tugs, never like this. He was rushed to the veterinarian, where X-rays were taken, and it was discovered that he had severely injured his back and spine. The prognosis was not good. Megan was inconsolable.

Smiley lay with braces and on painkillers. He was scheduled to start aqua therapy the next week, but the swelling in his back had to go down before proceeding. He always was a trooper, and everyone at the rehab center loved him. Sometimes you would see him grinning and blitzed from the meds. Each day, once the swelling had gone down, Smiley swam. He would float in his lemon-yellow life preserver, and every once in a while he would yip to be sure everyone heard him. There he was, suspended in the trough, with a life preserver with little rings that held him up. Smiley was actually enjoying this after he got the "hang" of it! He paddled his tiny legs, enjoying the attention. But Meg wondered if he was just being brave and trying to hide the pain. It would not be okay to have Smiley W living in pain. Weeks and weeks passed, and he had to remain on large doses of pain medication. He would come home after his aqua therapy and speak to all the others:

"Hi! I'm home. I went to the private swimming pool today. They love me, and I am sure that I will be better. They say that I am a tough guy!"

MooMoo darted a response: "Just how do you know what they say? You are deaf! You probably don't hear me, either."

"Then why are you blabbing? Smiley can hear us when he wants to!" said Cherish to her obnoxious little son.

Interestingly, Smiley was probably able to sense things well beyond what they all would have thought. He kept eating well and went everywhere with Megan and Sam now. He was treated like royalty and lay like a baby cradled in Meg's arms when they went to the restaurant for lunch on the deck. He gazed around, and she almost knew that he was aware he was holding court for all of the guests.

"Wow, look at me! I float!"

He was extremely sweet, and with those big ears…everyone came over to him.

One day Megan and Sam were in the greenhouse and had brought Smiley out to spend some time with them. In the greenhouse, Smiley had company. Scruff, who was always afraid of these monsters, had kept his distance, but now, very slowly, he crept up to Smiley.

"Are you one of these monsters? Who are you?" he bravely queried Smiley. "You haven't chased me."

Smiley, sensing the company, answered, "I am Smiley W. I don't need to chase you. It would be impossible. I can sense you, but I cannot see you."

The small wheelbarrow of potting soil was near Megan and Sam so that they could fill the pots for the orchid transplants they were working on. Sam set Smiley up in the wheelbarrow where she could watch him. All of a sudden, the unmistakable signs of little "Smiley Devil" and his bold side came to light again!

"Look at me. In this bucket…with real dirt again! I think I deserve treats!" He barked and barked as his tail wagged. He was rooting through the soil that was being thrown through the air and onto the worktable, Sam, and the pups below. Oreo sneezed. MooMoo shook and shook to get the dirt out of his coat. Cherish looked up at Smiley and concluded:

"I guess you must feel better. You're back in trouble again!" Coco stayed far away, and Miss Beau stood with her very tiny paws on Sam, begging to come up and out of the dirt fog. This was a good day!

"Oops! Too much dirt below!"

The Holiday Season is Coming

A few months later, arrangements were in shades of red now, as the Christmas season was upon them. The house was being decorated, and the pups naturally were in the middle of the trimmings! Coco was buried in the ribbons. "Don't I look gorgeous?" she pranced. MooMoo had the shiny popcorn string out of the box and was running around the tables with the string draped over everything but the tree.

"Will you just leave it, Moo Moo! I am caught in this string, and now how do I get out?" she wondered if anyone would listen. Miss Beau was trimmed totally as it looped around her. Smiley was sitting on the sideline, as he knew they all would be in trouble soon. He felt the breeze as MooMoo ran past, brushing by him. Cherish lay under the Christmas tree. She gazed at the lights and, as usual, was taken by the twinkling. Megan sat by the tree as Sam poured the wine. Each pup had a sip of eggnog, and it covered their noses. They pigged out on the raw veggies that the girls had made to have with dip.

"Veggies, what do they think we are, Rabbits?" Moo complained loudly. "Ribs would have been nice!"

The music was on, and Christmas songs rang in the holiday spirit. Megan and Sam turned

"Let me loose, MooMoo!"

to trim the tree, taking the popcorn string away from MooMoo. "I don't know why they need it. It looks better on us!" he asserted. Totally engrossed with placing each ornament with orchids in the perfect position, they forgot the food for a second. They turned as suddenly there was a splash. There was Smiley with his head and front paws in the eggnog bowl. His face was covered with eggnog, and a couple of chunks of cheese were floating on top. He looked so proud of himself. Cherish looked over and barked,

"You total little fool. I'm going to have to clean you off now!" She strutted over to the low table and jumped up to join Smiley to be sure that she would be the one to clean off the eggnog.

Getting there, she knocked into the bowl, and over it went. Now everyone was covered, including the floor! Megan and Sam just looked in disbelief. *How can these little dogs get into so much mischief?* they asked themselves.

"It must be totally food-motivated, as they are usually lazy louts right about now!" Sam said in the midst of laughing. "It's a good thing that we have the wine!"

Then Santa came, and the dogs all received lots of toys. Smiley received his toys plus a new coat that was made especially for him with hot and cold packs in it. Depending upon the soreness, he could enjoy his compresses for hours with its help. He tried it on.

"Look at my new coat! It even has my name on it!" he boasted, but Cherish, being the oldest of the crew, really thought it should be hers. There was a matching blanket to go with the special coat, and every time Smiley moved, Cherish burrowed a hole to lie in the middle of the blanket and flopped down. They all slept around the new bed with the fireplace burning by the corner.

"Smiley, you little fool!" YUM!

Christmas Is Here!

Christmas Day was amazing, as the family went to the beach and sat on the docks. The dogs saw seals for the very first time, and Megan and Sam had all they could do to hold the five dogs back. They yipped and barked, and their tails wagged. "I really wonder what they are thinking?" Sam said.

The boats were on the water even at Christmas. At sundown, there was a special Christmas celebration on the water where all of the boats were laden with decorations and lights. The girls had brought treats for everyone, and they found a great restaurant for themselves along the docks with a view of the harbor. The group definitely drew a crowd as the four very decked-out dachshunds and the very furry little Beau were sitting around the table on the floor begging. Coca, Cherish, and Beau had fancy woven collars laced with red orchids and bells. MooMoo and Smiley had bright red and green neck scarves with little antlers on their heads. Smiley sat tall with his new coat filled with a cool pack. He really was "All That." The lights glistened in the water, and the sky reflected clouds in the night, all through the light of the moon.

The holiday week was busy at the greenhouse, and New Year's was soon upon them. Sam and Megan thanked God that Smiley had been happy and healthy for another Christmas. He had been with Megan for eleven Christmases now!!! The following Tuesday, Smiley went back to the rehab center to continue his swimming.

He was not into swimming that day and mostly just floated in his tank with the life preserver and floats lying against him. "He must be tired today. All of the dogs have had a very tiring holiday. They're really getting older now," Megan said to the therapist.

"Give him a few days' rest, and make an appointment for next week," the therapist said. "That would be the second week of January." Megan agreed and made the appointment.

The house was eerie quiet that night, as Meg was terrified that they were running out of time. It was true that all the dogs had been whupped by the holidays and were laid out by the fireplace. Smiley lay on the quilt next to Oreo. A friendly face came down and licked Smiley's nose and face. Smiley looked up to "see" Honey Bunny. A Honey Bunny with wings!

"Wow, you really did get wings, Honey. I knew you would. Are you coming back to us? Please, please, please!! I miss you!" he told her.

"No, Smiley, it's time to come with me. We really need your help," Honey said.

"But I can't leave my Oreo and my family. I want my Momma Cherish and Momma Megan and Sam and…well, everyone," Smiley protested.

"Smiley, they will all join you in time. Your job is done here, but you are so special that God is calling you. And, by the way, yes, I have wings, and, yes, I am an Angel. It's time

Smiley. Come." That night Smiley was lifted to foreverdom. He floated with Honey, looking back sadly.

"Remember, Smiley, all you have to do is believe. You are still there for them. They will even be able to see you in their everyday things," he heard a voice telling him. Smiley was confused. But something was coming over him. He went over the clouds, and just beyond he SAW the lush green meadow and all of the angels. He saw Choco and Grey Boy.

"I really am seeing you all again…. Wait, I am SEEING you and HEARING you, too!" he cried out. "I don't hurt anymore, and I feel like a young pup again. Better than ever!"

"This is your world now, Smiley W, and this is Heaven," the Honey Angel told him. "You will have your special assignments and will be sent to help those that need you most. God sends us to help. That is why God created dogs, and we are definitely dogs."

Thinking of all his other welcome changes, Smiley looked at Honey and hesitantly asked, "How are my ears? Did they shorten? Are they normal?"

Honey looked at Smiley. "Your ears are the same. They are yours for a reason. That was your endearing quality. Love those ears, as they were your wings on earth." Then Honey and Smiley romped through the lush flower-filled pastures without even a bee to sting their noses. The smell of the flowers and the clear fresh air filled all the space around them.

"I guess this really is Heaven," Smiley said, happily.

"Smiley...come with me."

On awaking, Megan leaned over to see Smiley lying on his bed wrapped in his special coat. She leaned down and then lay beside him, feeling his little head and snuggling those gorgeous ears, knowing that Smiley had passed. Of all the hurt Megan had felt, she knew this was going to be unbearable. She and Sam cried and cried and begged God to return Smiley. They continued to mourn, and then Megan heard a voice:

"Remember, we are only apart for a while. We will be here for you. All you have to do is believe. Please believe."

A week later, Smiley came down with wings and took Oreo.

A seemingly lost family is waiting patiently to see their loved ones. They continue their day-to-day life, making the very best of every day with Coco, MooMoo, Miss Beau, and Momma Cherish. Every night just before closing their eyes, Megan prays:

"To Smiley and Oreo, Honey and Choco, Grey Boy and Mom, and all of our loved ones…. Be well, and we will see you soon!"

At times now when things get tough and they lack strength, they look to the sky, and there is Smiley, with his wings, and they know he is telling them…. "Just believe."

The End